Kiddo-napped?

Oliver dashed desperately around the shed. "Oh, no!" he said to himself. "The Raiders *are* trying to steal Kiddo the goat away from the home team, the Tigers! *And* they picked Dishwasher Donnelly to be the mascot's thief!"

The Raider was peeking around to the front of the shed and taking bites out of a hot dog. He wiped his hand on his jersey, leaving a big mustard smear mixed with sauerkraut!

Convinced that he'd lured Oliver away, the Dishwasher charged into Kiddo's shed. "Ah-ha!" he cried. "I gotcha!"

But Kiddo had other ideas!

GETTING OLIVER'S GOAT

MICHAEL McBRIER

Illustrated by Blanche Sims

Troll Associates

Library of Congress Cataloging in Publication Data

McBrier, Michael.
    Getting Oliver's goat.

    Summary: Oliver's new job, taking care of an
unpredictable goat, jeopardizes his chances of
winning the big bicycle race.
    [1. Goats—Fiction.   2. Bicycles and bicycling—
Fiction]   I. Sims, Blanche, ill.   II. Title.
PZ7.M47828G2   1988   [Fic]   87-13870
ISBN 0-8167-1145-3 (lib. bdg.)
ISBN 0-8167-1146-1 (pbk.)

A TROLL BOOK, published by Troll Associates,
Mahwah, NJ 07430

GETTING OLIVER'S GOAT

CHAPTER
1

Screech, *squeak, rattle. Screech, squeak, rattle.*

"Not *again!*" Oliver Moffitt groaned as he listened to the weird sounds his old five-speed bike was making. "This is starting to drive me crazy!"

"That bike does sound a little sick," Samantha Lawrence laughed from the bicycle next to him. Sam was Oliver's best friend and next-door neighbor. She and Oliver were on their way to the junior high school for a pep rally and football game.

"*Sick* isn't the word for it," replied Oliver gloomily. "This bike's ready for the junk heap!" He watched Sam glide past him. She grinned as she hunched over the handlebars of her new bright-blue ten-speed.

Suddenly Sam shouted, "Watch out! Pothole ahead!" She steered expertly around the giant hole.

But the screeches and squeaks were too loud for Oliver to hear her. And he was too busy flipping gears and pedaling hard to see if he could make the noises stop. The first time he realized the hole was there was when he crashed right into it.

"H-h-hey, S-S-Sam!" Oliver rattled his way across rocks and bumped over huge clumps of asphalt paving. "H-h-h-help!"

Sam zoomed back just as Oliver bounced out of the hole and wobbled to a stop. "Are you okay?" she asked.

Oliver nodded slowly. Then he wiped some beads of sweat off his forehead with his jacket sleeve. It was very warm for late September. "Whew!" he said. "That was worse than the Shake 'n' Quake ride at the Fireman's Fair!"

"Are you kidding?" said Sam. "That's one of my favorite rides!" She got back on her bike. "Come on, we don't want to be late for the pep rally."

They rode on in silence. This time Oliver kept a sharp lookout for potholes. There weren't any in sight, and he began to relax.

"You're really lucky your birthday's in June," he said to Sam. "You got your ten-speed just in time for the bike-a-thon," he sighed. "My birthday's not for months yet. And I need a new bike *now*!"

Sam turned and stared at him. "Does that mean you're not going to enter the race?" She looked back at the road just in time to avoid crashing into a couple of garbage cans. "Oops," she said. "That was a close one!"

"You can say that again," muttered Oliver. He'd just barely missed hitting the garbage cans too. The ride through the pothole had loosened up his handlebars. Now he was having a tough time steering.

"Why don't you just fix up your bike?" Sam said. "Then you could ride it in the race."

"I've *tried*," said Oliver. "But it's just too old. Besides, I'm not as good with machines as I am with animals."

Oliver loved animals and knew how to take care of them. In fact, he was the only kid he knew who had his own pet-care business. His motto was "I'm good with dogs and good with cats. I'll even baby-sit your rats!" He hadn't come across any pet rats yet. But he *had* taken care of a duck, a camel, and an alligator. And frankly, he thought they were a lot more fun than bicycles.

Sam shook her head. "Well, it won't be any fun if you don't race too. The bike-a-thon is the biggest event of the year. Only fifth and sixth graders can enter it. And Ms. Callahan was hoping for a good turnout from our class. . . ." Ms. Callahan was their teacher at Bartlett Woods Elementary School.

Oliver sighed. "It's an eight-mile race," he said. "With this dumb bike, I'd probably get about half a mile from the starting line, and then my wheels would fall off. Uh-oh," he said suddenly, as his bike started wobbling again. "I shouldn't have said that."

"Why not?" asked Sam.

"I think my wheel's coming off *now*." Oliver stopped and got off his bicycle.

"Oh, just tighten it up." Sam dug out the wrench from the tool kit she always carried on her bike. "I still think you should race. It's for charity. And the winner and runner-up each get a silver trophy in the shape of a bicycle. I think that's really neat!"

Oliver rolled his eyes. "Sure. *You* think it's neat because you'll probably *win* it!" Sam was the best athlete in their class. In fact, she was a better athlete than most of the kids at Bartlett Woods. The whole school had been talking about the bike-a-thon for days. It was taking place in two weeks. Everyone figured either Sam or Rusty Jackson, a sixth grader, was going to win. Nobody was rooting for Rusty. He was the meanest, sneakiest kid in school. He was also Oliver's sworn enemy.

"If you had a new bike, I bet you could beat Rusty," said Sam. "Then we'd be winner and runner-up. Maybe we could even tie!"

Oliver knew Sam was just being nice. Even with a new bike, he didn't think he'd be able to tie up the race with her. And he wasn't so sure about beating Rusty either. But with a new bike, at least he'd have a *chance*.

Oliver finished his repairs and gave back the wrench. "I saw the greatest bike down at Bobb's Bikearama," he told Sam. "It's a red Grafton Deluxe ten-speed. But even at the special sale price, it's still too expensive."

"Even with the money you've saved up from your business?" Sam said.

"It's just not enough. My mom said she'd lend me the rest of the money if I could promise to pay her back. But business is terrible right now. There just aren't any customers." Oliver shook his head.

"Mrs. Kessler even called me up last night to say she wouldn't need me to take care of her cat, Ralphie-Boy," said Oliver. "She's decided not to go on that two-week cruise after all." He sighed. "I guess I'm just not very lucky these days."

Oliver and Sam pedaled toward the corner of Sutherland Avenue and Church Street. In the distance, Oliver could see the junior high school. Suddenly Sam stopped short. Oliver screeched to a halt beside her. "What's going on?" he demanded. "Why did you stop?"

"I just had an idea," Sam said.

"What idea?" Oliver asked wearily. He had been pedaling in all five gears just to keep up with Sam.

Sam bit her lip and looked at Oliver, her eyes gleaming. "How about a practice race—a sort of mini bike-a-thon—right now? Just between you and me. From here to the first fence post of the school."

"You want to race *now*?" Oliver rolled his eyes.

"Sure!" said Sam. "Why not? I mean, you've never raced that bike before, right?"

"Right." Oliver nodded.

"So you don't *really* know what it can do, right?"

12

Oliver shook his head doubtfully. "You're right. I don't know what this bike can do," he agreed, "but I sure know what it *can't* do!"

"Come on," Sam coaxed. "What have you got to lose?"

Oliver thought for a minute, then shrugged. "Okay. I'll give it a try. But we'd better start from the light." He pointed to the corner. "See, it's just changed to red. When it turns green, you yell 'Go!' and we'll take off."

Sam nodded approvingly. "That's a good plan. I can see you're getting into the racing spirit already."

Oliver didn't know about that, but he figured that since he'd agreed to race Sam, the two of them might as well do things right.

"Okay," said Sam. They rode to the corner and lined up their bikes next to each other. "Get ready. The light's going to change any minute now." She leaned over the handlebars and looked at him. "There's just one more thing."

"What's that?" asked Oliver as he stared at the light.

"Forget it's me you're racing. Pretend I'm your worst enemy, the guy you have to beat. Make believe I'm *Rusty Jackson!*"

"Did I hear someone mention my name?"

Oliver and Sam turned around. Rusty Jackson and his friend Jay Goodman were standing right behind them. Rusty was flashing his nastiest grin.

"Talking about me behind my back, Moffitt?" Rusty asked in a mean voice.

Before Oliver could answer, Sam said coldly, "I was talking, not Oliver. And anyway, we're in front of your back, not behind it."

Rusty narrowed his eyes. "Is that supposed to be a joke or something?"

"You wouldn't know a joke if it ran up and punched you in the nose," said Sam.

"Hey, then you'd get a punch line!" Jay added. "Get it? A *punch* line! Ha! Ha! Ha!"

Sam rolled her eyes and shook her head slowly.

"Shut up, Jay," Rusty growled. "Don't be a jerk."

Jay immediately stopped laughing.

Oliver groaned silently. At this rate, he and Sam would never get their minirace over with, let alone make it to the game.

"Look, Rusty," he said, trying to sound calm. "Sam and I were just about to race each other over to the junior high. Sort of a mini bike-a-thon. So would you guys mind getting lost?"

Rusty looked at Jay with raised eyebrows. Then he looked at Oliver and began to laugh. "Now, that's a *real* joke!" he hooted. "You're going to race Sam on *that* hunk of junk?" He jerked a thumb in the direction of Oliver's bike and laughed even louder. Jay laughed with him. This time Rusty didn't tell him to shut up. Oliver felt his face grow warm.

"You won't think it's so funny when Oliver beats you by a mile in the bike-a-thon!" shouted Sam.

Now it was Oliver's turn to raise his eye-

brows. "Hey, wait a minute, Sam," he warned. "Remember, I told you I didn't think I was going to enter . . ."

"Beat me? No way," sneered Rusty. He glanced at Oliver's bike, then looked down at his own bike and gave a short laugh. He patted the leather seat lovingly. Oliver noticed that Rusty's bike was a black Grafton ten-speed, the super-deluxe model. Oliver knew it was one of the sleekest and best racing bikes around. Next to Rusty's bike, Oliver's little five-speed looked like a tricycle.

"How about putting your money where your mouth is, old sport?" Rusty said suddenly. "I challenge you and that junk-yard-on-wheels to a race. Just the two of us. Here and now. From the stoplight to the first fence post. Okay?"

Oliver didn't know what to say. He knew his bike would never beat Rusty's. But if he refused Rusty's challenge, he'd look like a coward. He made a quick decision. After all, his honor was at stake.

"Okay." Oliver nodded. "Let's go."

Sam moved aside so that Rusty could take her place next to Oliver. "Good luck," she whispered. "I'm rooting for you."

"Thanks," Oliver muttered. He didn't add "for getting me into this mess in the first place."

Jay took charge. "Okay, racers," he said importantly. "When the light turns green again, I'll yell 'Go!' Ready, set . . ."

Oliver made sure his handlebars were straight. Then he leaned over them and gritted his teeth.

"Okay, bike," he muttered. "Don't let me down *now!*"

"Go!" yelled Jay.

Oliver started to pump with all his might. He and Rusty rode neck-and-neck across the intersection.

"Come on!" shouted Sam. "Don't let him take the lead!"

"I'm trying, I'm trying!" Oliver shouted back. He looked up and saw Rusty glide past him, his hands clasped behind his head.

"Look, Moffitt. No hands," Rusty called out.

Oliver frantically flipped gears and pedaled harder, trying to catch up. But it was no use. His bike was too creaky and slow, and Rusty was far ahead of him now. Oliver saw Jay and Sam ride past. In a few seconds they caught up to Rusty. "Oh, great," Oliver muttered. "They're not even racing!"

Finally Oliver managed to make it to the fence post, where Rusty, Jay, and Sam were waiting for him.

Oliver screeched to a stop, puffing and gasping. It had been a tough ride. A *slow,* tough ride. His legs were shaky from all the hard pumping he'd done. His arms were stiff from holding the handlebars tightly.

"Face it, Moffitt," Rusty said in a bored voice. "You're a loser. There's no way you could ever beat me. Not today, not in the bike-a-thon, not *ever!*" He and Jay started to walk their bikes through the gate leading to the junior high football field.

"Don't pay any attention to him," said Sam. "You know what a jerk he is. I'll win the bike-a-thon for both of us."

But Oliver shook his head. "No way," he said. "I'm going to beat that creep. All I need is a new bike, and a customer to pay for it. And when I find one, watch out, Rusty Jackson!"

CHAPTER
2

"Wow, this place is really packed," said Sam as she and Oliver headed toward the football field. "I'll bet everybody is rooting for the Tigers too." The Tigers was the name of the junior high football team.

Oliver didn't say anything.

"You know, this is a really important game," Sam continued. "If the Tigers beat the Raiders today, they'll be closer than ever to the county championship."

Oliver just shrugged. He didn't feel like talking about the crowd or the Tigers' chances for the county championship. He just wanted to go home and figure out a way to make some money and buy a new bike. Every time he closed his eyes, he kept seeing Rusty's mean grin and hearing his mocking voice. Oliver imagined himself tossing Rusty and Rusty's bike into a garbage can. Rusty was begging for mercy. Oliver was just about to close the lid—

Oliver's daydream was interrupted by a poke from Sam.

"Hey, there's Josh and the gang!" she shouted, pointing to the home-team bleachers. "Oh, wow, they have great seats too! Come on!" She took off through the crowd. Oliver jogged after her.

When they got to the bleachers, Oliver saw his friends and classmates, Josh Burns, Matthew Farley, Jennifer Hayes, and Kimberly Williams.

Josh was sitting in the second row. He was holding a huge bag of popcorn. "What happened to you guys?" he asked. "We thought you got lost or something."

Oliver and Sam squeezed onto the seat between Josh and Matthew.

"We didn't get lost," Oliver said. "We ran into Rusty Jackson." He told Josh about his race with Rusty.

When Oliver had finished, Josh held out the popcorn bag. "Have some popcorn," he offered. "You look like you could use it."

Oliver and Sam each took a handful and started to munch.

"Rusty's acting like a big shot just because he has the only new Grafton Super-Deluxe ten-speed in school," Josh said.

Oliver frowned. "Rusty acts like a big shot about *everything*," he reminded Josh.

"Well, he's big all right," giggled Sam. "A big pain!"

Josh started to laugh. Oliver grinned. He suddenly felt better than he had all day.

"What's so funny?" demanded Matthew Farley, leaning across Oliver. Matthew was the smallest kid in their class.

Jennifer Hayes and Kim Williams, who were sitting in the first row, turned around. Jennifer was wearing a purple suede jacket with dark purple fringes. She was also wearing an enormous pair of purple sunglasses. On one temple-piece was the word *Purple*. On the other was the word *Worms*. The Purple Worms was Jennifer's favorite rock group.

"You guys sound like a convention of hyenas," she said, peering at them over the top of her sunglasses.

"Hyenas!" exclaimed Kim. "That reminds me." She tapped Oliver on the knee. "I was supposed to give you a message from Parnell." Parnell was Kim's big brother. He was the captain of the Tigers.

"Hyenas remind you of Oliver?" Josh laughed.

"No. When Jennifer mentioned hyenas, it reminded me of animals," Kim explained, "which reminded me that I was supposed to ask you if you wanted a job taking care of one."

"A hyena?" Oliver stared at Kim, totally confused.

"No, silly!" replied Kim. "An animal."

Oliver's eyes lit up. He couldn't believe his luck. This just might be the solution to his problem. "Tell me more," he said to Kim.

Kim popped a stick of bubble gum into her

mouth, chewed for a moment, and blew a huge pink bubble. Then she said, "The Tigers have a new team mascot. And Parnell wants you to take care of it for the whole football season. That's all I know."

"That's great!" cried Oliver. "I'll take the job! How much does it pay? When do I start?"

Kim shook her head and shrugged. "Don't ask me," she said. "Ask Parnell. He wants to talk to you about it after the game."

Oliver sat back and smiled happily. He could relax. Now he would be able to buy his new bike and race against Rusty in the bike-a-thon. His troubles were over.

Suddenly Kim gave Oliver a nudge and pointed toward the field. "Look, there's Parnell."

Oliver looked toward the sidelines. Parnell was standing there, dressed in his football uniform. "Blue and Gold!" Kim cheered. Those were the Tigers' colors.

Standing a few feet away from Parnell was the biggest kid Oliver had ever seen. He was wearing a red and white Raiders uniform.

"Uh-oh," Kim said in a low, serious voice. "It's the Dishwasher."

"The *what*?" asked Oliver.

"Not *what*," corrected Kim. "*Who*. Dilbert Washburn Donnelly. He's a tackle for the Raiders. He got the nickname 'The Dishwasher' because he 'cleans up the offense and drowns the defense.' "

Oliver stared at Dishwasher Donnelly. He was holding four hot dogs dripping with mustard and sauerkraut in one huge hand. In the other hand was a jumbo-sized plastic bottle of soda. Oliver and his friends watched as the Dishwasher wolfed down the hot dogs. In between bites he took big gulps of soda.

"His nickname should be 'The Slob,' " sniffed Jennifer.

Just then Oliver saw Parnell wave at him to come over. Oliver smiled, waved back, and nodded.

"What's up?" Oliver asked after he had jogged over to Parnell. "Kim said you wanted to talk to me after the game."

Parnell nodded. "I know. But I really need your help now. The pep rally is going to start any minute, and I need someone to lead our mascot onto the field. Norman Willis, the coach's son, was supposed to do it, but he had to go home. And since you're the best animal person in town . . ."

"I'll be happy to fill in." Oliver grinned. "Where is he?"

Parnell gave a loud whistle, and one of his teammates came out from under the bleachers. He held one end of a long rope. On the other end was—

"A goat?" said Oliver.

The goat came trotting up to Parnell. He was wearing a blue and gold banner that said TIGERS.

"Oliver, meet Kiddo," Parnell said, grabbing hold of the goat's rope. "Kiddo, meet Oliver."

Oliver patted the black and white goat on the head. He was careful to avoid the two sharp

horns. "Hi, Kiddo," he said. He took the rope from Parnell.

"Thanks," said Parnell. "I knew you wouldn't let us down!"

"*Slurrpp!*" Someone was loudly finishing a soda right behind them.

Oliver and Parnell whirled around and almost bumped into Dishwasher Donnelly. Oliver noticed that the Dishwasher's uniform was covered with mustard smears.

Suddenly the Raiders' coach stomped up. "What are you doing here, Donnelly?" he asked angrily. "You're supposed to be warming up with the rest of the team!"

"Aw, gimme a break, Coach," whined the Dishwasher. "I had to have my pregame snack. You know I can't play on an empty stomach. I gotta keep up my strength!"

The angry coach led Dishwasher Donnelly back toward the Raiders' bench. But Oliver noticed the Dishwasher glancing back sneakily over his shoulder. "Why's that guy giving us funny looks?" Oliver asked.

Parnell looked worried. "I heard a rumor that the Raiders are planning to steal Kiddo away from us," he said.

Oliver opened his eyes wide. "Steal Kiddo?" he asked. "But why?"

"Kiddo was the Raiders' mascot last year when they won the county championship," Parnell explained. "This year they had a dancing kangaroo, but he got sick. We got Kiddo before they could get to him. Now they're afraid Kiddo will bring us the same good luck he brought them last year!"

Before Oliver could ask Parnell if he thought the Dishwasher was the one who planned to steal Kiddo, the school marching band began to play. They marched onto the field and arranged themselves into a "T" shape.

"I'd better get back to the team," said Parnell. "Just be prepared to lead Kiddo onto the field." He ran off.

"Hey, wait a minute," Oliver shouted after him. "When do I lead Kiddo onto the—"

Just then, the band struck up a chorus of "Old MacDonald Had a Farm."

Kiddo jerked up his head and took off onto the field, dragging Oliver behind him.

"Stop, Kiddo, stop!" Oliver puffed. But the goat kept on running. He was headed right for the marching band. Just before Kiddo reached them, the band stopped playing. And Kiddo stopped too—right in his tracks.

Oliver, running frantically with the rope in his hands, didn't see Kiddo stop. He went on for three more steps, crashing into a majorette, who crashed into a tuba player.

"Hellllp!" yelled the tuba player, losing his balance. He fell on top of the glockenspiel player who stood behind him. She shrieked and fell onto the clarinet player in back of her. One by one, all the band members lost their balance and fell on top of one another.

"Get off me, kid!" ordered the tuba player, giving Oliver a shove. The other band members

27

muttered angrily as they struggled to their feet, clutching their instruments. Oliver could hear the crowd laughing and cheering. The cheerleaders were pointing to Oliver and Kiddo and laughing too.

Oliver looked at Kiddo and sighed. The goat was busy chewing on some grass. He looked very pleased with himself.

It was a short pep rally. After it was over, the two competing football teams started to run onto the field.

"Uh-oh," said Oliver. "Game time." He tugged at Kiddo's leash. "Come on, Kiddo, let's go." But the goat didn't want to leave. He was too happy nibbling on the grass.

Oliver pulled harder, but Kiddo wouldn't budge. Then Oliver dropped Kiddo's leash and jogged over to the band. They all gave him looks.

"Look, would you guys mind playing 'Old MacDonald' again?" he gulped. "My goat—" Before Oliver could finish his sentence, the band started to play the song. And Kiddo ran off the field at top speed.

"Oh, no, not *again!*" cried Oliver as he sprinted after the goat. People quickly jumped aside as Kiddo, with Oliver in hot pursuit, charged past them.

Finally Oliver caught up with Kiddo by the hot dog stand. The goat had stopped and was sniffing at some hot dog wrappers careless fans had thrown onto the ground. Oliver grabbed Kiddo's leash and held it tightly.

"Is your goat in training for the Kentucky Derby?" asked the hot dog salesman.

"Not *this* goat," Oliver replied firmly. "From now on, his racing days are *over*."

After the game Oliver and Kiddo were standing at the entrance to the locker room. Parnell came out and showed Oliver the shed he and his teammates had built for Kiddo. It looked a little lopsided to Oliver, but he didn't say anything.

"Having a team mascot was my idea," Parnell explained. "Kiddo comes from MacDonald's Petting Farm. The Raiders were ready to kick themselves when I got there before they did!"

Oliver felt Kiddo gently butt him on the leg. "Cut it out, Kiddo." He moved a few inches away from the goat. Kiddo moved back to Oliver's side, put his wet nose into Oliver's hand, and started sniffing. Oliver snatched his hand away and wiped it on his jeans.

"He likes you." Parnell beamed. "I can tell." He opened the door of the shed and pointed to some bags in the corner. "That's Kiddo's food," he said. "It's a mixture called Sweet Feed."

Oliver nodded. "*Zoo World* did a show on goats a few weeks ago," he told Parnell. "I took notes." *Zoo World* was Oliver's favorite TV program. He always took notes when he watched it, even during the programs on animals like wart hogs and anteaters.

"Goats are really easy to take care of," Oliver continued. "They just have to be given food and

water twice a day. And they like carrots and apples as treats."

"I knew you were the man for the job." Parnell grinned. "Actually, I'd take care of Kiddo myself, but all my free time is taken up with football practice. Our team really wants to win the county championship this year. And with our win today, we're only four games away from the final!"

Oliver felt something in his jacket pocket. He looked down. Kiddo again! The goat snagged a bag of salted peanuts Oliver had brought as a snack. Before Oliver could stop him, the peanuts were gone—wrapper and all. Kiddo chewed happily.

Oliver remembered the woman on *Zoo World* saying that goats like to sniff out and chew on anything that is salty.

"So, are you going to take the job?" Parnell wanted to know.

For a minute Oliver wasn't sure. He thought Kiddo might be something of a handful. "How much will you pay me?" he asked doubtfully.

Parnell named the amount. Oliver gasped. It was more money than he'd ever made before. He would be able to pay his mother back, and he would still have some money left over. It was definitely an offer he couldn't refuse.

But Oliver suddenly thought of something else.

"What about the Raiders' plan to steal Kiddo?" he asked. "Do you think it's for real?"

Parnell shrugged. "Could be. We can't take

any chances. Just make sure the shed is locked up tight when you leave. And I'll ask Mr. Grobie, the school security guard, to keep an eye on Kiddo at night."

"Okay." Oliver grinned. "I'll take the job!"

"Great!" said Parnell. "Here's the key to the shed. I've got to get along. Team meeting. See you later!" He ran off.

Oliver led his new client gently but firmly into the shed, gave him some Sweet Feed, and made sure he had plenty of water.

"Kiddo," he told the goat, "you just became my ticket to the bike-a-thon." Oliver gave Kiddo a pat on the head. Kiddo rubbed against him. Then he began bolting down the bowl of Sweet Feed.

Oliver was about to close and lock the shed when he heard something. It sounded like pebbles rattling against the back of the shed.

Oliver froze. Was someone hanging around, waiting for a chance to steal Kiddo? "You stay here," he whispered to Kiddo. "I'll take a look around."

He tiptoed out the door and crept around to the back of the shed. Peeking around the corner, he saw—nothing.

"I could have sworn I heard something," Oliver said to himself. He searched behind the shed, but nobody was around.

Shrugging his shoulders, Oliver walked around the corner—and nearly crashed into a broad back in a red and white jersey—a Raider uniform!

The Raider was peeking around to the front of

the shed and taking big bites out of a hot dog with extra sauerkraut he'd been holding. He wiped his hand on his jersey, leaving a big mustard smear.

There could be no doubt—this could only be Dishwasher Donnelly!

Convinced that he'd lured Oliver away, the Dishwasher charged into Kiddo's shed. "Ah-ha!" he cried. "I gotcha!"

CHAPTER
3

Oliver dashed desperately around the shed. "Oh, no," he said to himself. "The Raiders *are* trying to steal Kiddo. And they picked Dishwasher Donnelly to be the thief!"

"Gotcha!" the Dishwasher roared again. "Gotcha-cha-a-CHOO!" Oliver reached the door and stopped short. There was Dishwasher Donnelly, wiping his nose on the sleeve of his jersey. He ran toward Kiddo, grabbed for him, and sneezed. Then he stood up, wiped his nose again, and tried to grab Kiddo again. And once more he sneezed.

"Hold—*hah-choo!*—still!" said the Dishwasher. "I'm gonna—*ge-zzooosh!*—get you!"

Every time Dishwasher Donnelly came near the goat, he began sneezing his head off.

"I think you're allergic to him," Oliver said.

The Dishwasher whirled around. "Allergic,

shmallergic," he growled. "I'm gonna . . . AH-HAH-CHOO!"

Kiddo was right behind him. In fact, he was charging right into the Dishwasher's backside!

"Ah—yow!" The Dishwasher managed to sneeze and yell at the same time as Kiddo butted him right out of the shed. Oliver ducked as the football player went flying by.

Dishwasher Donnelly landed on the grassy lawn. He picked himself up, then bounded off toward the school parking lot without looking back.

"Good work, Kiddo," said Oliver. "I think he's allergic in more than one way now."

He closed the door, checked the lock, and walked toward the bike rack. He was worried. What if the Dishwasher tried to steal Kiddo again?

Then Oliver saw his old five-speed. Without this job he'd never be able to buy a new bike. He decided to forget about Dishwasher Donnelly.

"I'll sign up for the bike-a-thon," Oliver promised himself. "And then, look out, Rusty Jackson!"

Two days later Oliver was kneeling in the driveway outside his garage.

"Oliver Moffitt, come in here right now and finish your breakfast. That's an order!" Oliver's mother stood at the kitchen door. She had both hands on her hips and was tapping one foot impatiently.

"Okay, Mom, I'm coming." Oliver gave the

front tire of his new bike a final shot of air and screwed on the tire cap. Then he stood up and gazed admiringly at the shiny red Grafton Deluxe ten-speed.

Mrs. Moffitt's face softened. She knew how much Oliver loved his new bike.

"That bike certainly is a beauty," Mrs. Moffitt said as she and Oliver stepped into the kitchen.

"It's better than beautiful," Oliver sighed. "It's perfect." His mother had loaned him the money he needed to pay for it. Oliver was to pay her back with the money he earned taking care of Kiddo.

"You've been riding it a lot," said Mrs. Moffitt. "I guess you really enjoy it."

"I'm still getting used to it," Oliver admitted. "It's a lot harder shifting in ten gears instead of just five!"

"We could always get your old five-speed back and sell this one," teased Mrs. Moffitt.

"No way!" Oliver grinned.

Oliver sat down at the kitchen table and picked up his spoon. He'd been in the middle of a bite of corn flakes and strawberries, when he suddenly decided his front tire needed air. He frowned. Maybe it was the back tire, not the front, that needed some more air. He dropped his spoon and started to get up.

"Oliver," said his mother.

Oliver sat back down. That was his mother's "no nonsense, Oliver" tone. The back tire would have to wait. He took a strawberry out of the bowl and dangled it under his chair. Immediately it was snapped up by Pom-pom, Mrs. Moffitt's frisky little Shih Tzu. The little dog gave a yap. "Sorry," Oliver said. "Only one to a customer." He really wasn't supposed to feed Pom-pom from the table.

"By the way," said Mrs. Moffitt as she stuffed papers into her briefcase. "A week from Saturday I'm having the Kirkbys and the Caplans over for lunch. I'd really appreciate it if you could help me get everything ready."

Mrs. Moffitt worked as a bookkeeper at the Kirkby Insurance Agency. Oliver's parents had gotten divorced when Oliver was a baby. Oliver's father lived in another city.

"But, Mom, that's the day before the bike-a-thon!" Oliver exclaimed. "I'll have to get in some last-minute practicing!"

His mother nodded. "I know you will. That's why I'm giving you an advance warning. I need your help only in the morning. Then, after lunch, you're on your own."

Oliver wrinkled his forehead. "You mean I have to go to this lunch too?" He wasn't sure if he wanted to hang around with a bunch of grown-ups all afternoon. "I mean, I've got Kiddo to take care of, and there's the bike-a-thon, and—"

"I know, I know," said Mrs. Moffitt, smiling. "Just say hello to the Kirkbys and the Caplans and have something to eat. That's all I ask. Besides, Mrs. Kirkby is really looking forward to seeing you. You know how much she likes you."

Oliver grinned. "I like her too." Oliver had once taken care of Mrs. Kirkby's birds. He had to admit she was a pretty neat lady. Besides, he knew he couldn't let his mother down.

"Okay, Mom, I'm yours for a couple of hours on Saturday," he said. "Including a short appearance at lunch."

Mrs. Moffitt gave her son a quick hug. "I knew I could count on you." She zipped up her briefcase. "Now, let's get these breakfast dishes done. I've got to get to work, and you have to get to school!"

"I have to visit Kiddo first," Oliver reminded his mother. Every day, before and after school, Oliver rode over to Kiddo's shed to feed and water the goat. So far there hadn't been any sign of Dishwasher Donnelly. Oliver was pretty sure the Raiders had given up the idea of trying to steal Kiddo.

At least, he hoped they had.

"How's the job going, anyway?" Mrs. Moffitt wanted to know. She handed Oliver a clean dishtowel.

"Not too bad," replied Oliver. "But Kiddo can be kind of a pain sometimes. He loves to chew on my clothes, and he's always butting me. The walls of the shed are all splintered, too, because he likes to sharpen his horns on the wood."

Mrs. Moffitt's eyes twinkled. "In short, he's acting just like a goat," she said teasingly.

"That's for sure," sighed Oliver. He dried the last glass and placed it in the cabinet. "But I really can't complain," he added. "Thanks to Kiddo—and you—I've got my new bike." He sighed again. "I just wish I could ride it faster. At the rate I'm going, I'll never win the bike-a-thon."

"Whether you win or not," his mother said, "I know I'll be proud of you."

"Thanks, Mom." Oliver glanced at the clock. "Uh-oh, I'd better get over to Kiddo now, or I know one person who won't be proud of me— Ms. Callahan!" He grabbed his knapsack and ran out the door.

During recess Oliver studied the bulletin board next to the principal's office. On the board was a map showing the bike-a-thon route.

"I'm trying to memorize the route," he told Josh, who was standing next to him. "I figure that knowing the course really well will give me a head start."

"Good idea." Josh nodded. "That's what I'd do if I were racing. But I decided to drop out."

"How come?" Oliver asked.

Josh shrugged. "Too much practicing. I can't spare the time away from my computer." Sometimes Oliver wondered if that computer wasn't really Josh's best friend.

"Besides," Josh added mysteriously, "I came up with a better way to win the bike-a-thon. This way, I get all of the glory but none of the headaches. Want to hear my idea?"

"Sure." Oliver shrugged. "Why not?" He wished Josh would hurry up and explain. Recess was almost over, and Oliver wanted to take another look at the map. But Josh didn't waste any time getting to the point.

"How would you like a coach?" he asked Oliver. "I mean, how would you like me as your coach?"

"A coach!" Oliver exclaimed. "That's a great idea! I could really use the help. You could time my practice sprints, set up practice races, and give me encouragement." The more Oliver thought about it, the better he liked the idea. A coach was just what he needed.

Josh nodded enthusiastically. "Right. That's exactly what I'd do. And not only that, I found this great book on bike racing." He handed Oliver a large paperback book. Oliver read the title— Cycling to Win! Win! Win! Josh gave the book a tap. "With this book and my coaching there's no way you can lose that race."

"What're you doing, Moffitt?" said a nasty voice. "Checking the map to see where I'm gonna leave you in the dirt?"

Oliver and Josh turned around in time to see Rusty Jackson and Jay Goodman walk past them down the hall. They looked back at Oliver and laughed.

"I hear you got a new bike, pal," Rusty snickered. "But you still won't be able to beat me. Maybe you should ride that dumb goat you've been taking care of."

Jay's laughter rang in the hall as he and Rusty walked away.

Oliver turned to Josh. "So, when do we start training?" he asked.

"How about this afternoon?" Josh suggested. "I could set up a practice race after school between you, Sam, Matthew, Kim, and Jennifer. We'll race from here to the junior high. That way, we can all get to meet Kiddo, and you can get in some practicing."

Oliver grinned at Josh. "Sounds good to me, Coach," he said.

After school Josh marked out an imaginary starting line. Oliver and his friends lined up next to one another.

Oliver stuck his right foot onto the pedal and managed to fasten the special clamp over it. But he couldn't figure out how he was supposed to fasten the clamp onto his *left* foot without falling down.

"Ready," said Josh. "Set! *Go!*"

Oliver forgot about the other pedal and tried to concentrate on pumping as hard as he could. But he couldn't find the right gear. He looked up and saw Sam. She was about five feet in front of him. Then Josh passed him, followed by Kim, Jennifer, and Matthew.

"Oh, *no!*" Oliver groaned. "If *Matthew* can beat me, I'm in real trouble!"

Finally Oliver spotted the junior high school ahead. Then he saw the goal post, which was to be the finish line for the race. He glided through the goal post and braked to a stop.

"Whew," he heard Sam say. "That was some sprint!"

"Did I win?" asked Jennifer. Then she wailed, "Oh, no!" She bent over to look at the front fender of her purple ten-speed.

"Did you get a flat tire?" Sam asked.

"Worse! One of my Purple Worms decals came unstuck!" Jennifer poked at the peeling decal.

"I wouldn't worry about it," said Kim. "You've got nine left."

"But there are ten Purple Worms!" cried Jennifer. "It's just not the same at all!"

"Excuse me!" said Josh loudly. "Here are the results of the race. In last place—"

"Why don't you just tell us who came in first," Oliver interrupted quickly. Everybody had seen him ride through the goal post last.

"Well, the winner will be no surprise," Josh said. "It was Sam."

"You're right," replied Kim. "That isn't a surprise."

Oliver felt terrible. He wished he could have surprised everyone by beating Sam.

"Now I *know* you need a coach," Josh said to Oliver as they walked toward Kiddo's shed.

Oliver unlocked the door, and everybody stepped inside to take a look at Kiddo.

"He's kind of cute," Kim said. She gave Kiddo a gentle pat on the back.

"Hey, he has a little beard," Matthew laughed. "I guess he decided not to shave."

Oliver rolled his eyes. Matthew could really be dumb sometimes. "It's not called a beard, it's called a goatee," Oliver told him. "Most goats have them."

Kiddo liked all the attention he was getting. He stood quietly and let everyone pet him.

"This is where we keep his food," Oliver said, pointing to the bag of Sweet Feed. "He also eats carrots and apples. Anybody want to feed Kiddo a snack?"

"He's already eating one," said Josh.

"*Aaaaaaaaack!*" shrieked Jennifer. "He's got my new jacket!" Kiddo happily chewed on the purple suede fringes. His head bobbed up and down as Jennifer tried to shake loose.

"Make him stop! Make him stop!" she yelled.

Oliver tried to remove the fringes from Kiddo's mouth, but the goat wouldn't let go. He pulled on Jennifer's arm. Kiddo pulled back. It became a tug of war: Oliver and Jennifer on one side, Kiddo on the other.

"Okay, Jennifer, we'll pull together," said Oliver. "One . . . two . . . three!"

Kiddo let go of the fringe. Oliver and Jennifer tumbled onto the shed floor.

Oliver got up and reached into his jacket pocket for an apple. "Here, Kiddo. You'll like this much better than suede fringes." Kiddo took the apple and gobbled it up. All of it.

Jennifer stood up, dusting herself off. "That goat is a menace to well-dressed people," she complained. "I'm leaving." She tossed her head and stomped out the door.

Kim rolled her eyes and followed Jennifer outside.

"I have to go too," said Sam. "I've got a piano lesson this afternoon."

Josh and Matthew said that they had to leave too.

"I'll give you a call tonight," Josh said as he left. "We can talk about a training schedule."

After everyone had gone, Oliver picked up a small sack of Sweet Feed. He was about to pour the food into Kiddo's bowl, when he heard someone pounding on the door. The walls of the not-too-well-built shed shook.

"Knock, knock, anybody home?" said a high, phony voice.

Oliver stood with the sack in his hands. Kiddo butted him in the arm to remind him it was past his dinnertime.

The door opened, and Rusty and Jay stepped inside.

"What are you guys doing here?" Oliver asked. "Can't you see I'm busy?"

Jay ignored him. "Look at that dumb goat," he said.

"Which one?" asked Rusty. "The one with the horns or the one with the bag?"

Jay started laughing loudly.

Rusty walked up to Kiddo and pulled his goatee. Jay started to pull on Kiddo's horns.

"Hey, don't do that!" Oliver shouted. "Quit bothering him!"

Rusty gave Kiddo a sharp poke in the side.

"Who's gonna stop me, Moffitt?" he taunted. "You?"

He and Jay continued to tease Kiddo. But the goat didn't like being poked and pulled. He twisted his body around and tossed his head wildly to shake off Rusty and Jay.

"*Maaaa!*" he bawled. Then he leveled his head at Rusty and rammed into him. "Oof!" said Rusty.

Kiddo then turned around and butted Jay.

"Go, Kiddo!" Oliver muttered.

"Hey, Moffitt!" yelled Rusty. "Stop this dumb goat!" He and Jay ran out of the shed, slamming the door behind them.

Kiddo ran at the door and butted it hard. The whole shed shook.

"Kiddo, calm down!" Oliver yelled. But the goat was too angry. He kept butting the walls. The shed groaned and shook. Oliver heard Rusty's voice from behind the shed. "Nah, nah, ya stupid goat! You can't get us now!" Rusty and Jay started laughing.

Kiddo heard them too. He ran to the door, then rushed furiously at the back wall.

Wham! Kiddo hit the wall.

"Look out!" screamed Jay.

The back wall of the shed wobbled. It teetered. Then it fell down, pulling the roof down with it. Rusty and Jay stood frozen, staring.

Then the other walls collapsed. The sides flopped down. Finally the door crashed outward onto the grass.

Oliver grabbed Kiddo by the collar before he

could charge at Rusty again. "I know how you feel, but I can't let you do it," he said.

Over on the football field the Tigers had stopped practicing and were running for the shed.

"Let's get out of here!" yelled Rusty. He and Jay jumped on their bikes and hastily pedaled away.

Oliver stood very still, staring at the wreckage around him. Kiddo was calm now that Rusty and Jay were gone. He was nibbling contentedly on some Sweet Feed that had fallen out of one of the sacks.

"I don't believe this," Oliver said. "What more can go wrong?"

He stepped onto one of the side walls. "If I can pick this up, maybe I can push it back into place," he thought.

But as soon as he started walking across the wall, he heard a weird sound.

Ker-zoosh!

Oliver stopped and looked around. He couldn't see where the noise was coming from.

Kuh-huh-zoosh! It sounded like a muffled sneeze. Oliver bent over. *Zooosh!* It sounded as if it were coming from under his feet.

Oliver jumped back. The wall began moving!

Oof! Mmrrff! Ah-chooo!

Oliver stared in amazement as Dishwasher Donnelly slowly crawled out from under the collapsed wall. Wrapped around him was a huge net. Obviously this time the Dishwasher had

come prepared. But he hadn't been prepared for the wall falling on him.

"Uh, nice shed ya got here, kid," the Dishwasher said as he tore his way out of the net. Then he saw Kiddo snorting and lowering his horns. And beyond him he saw Parnell and the rest of the Tigers charging up. "Uh-oh, gotta get going."

With one final sneeze Dishwasher Donnelly sprinted off across the field. Oliver just managed to catch Kiddo's leash before he went charging after him. The Dishwasher looked more like a track star than a star tackle, he was running so fast!

Parnell and the team crowded around Oliver and Kiddo.

"What happened?" asked Parnell. "We were just leaving the locker room when we saw Kiddo's shed collapse. And wasn't that Dishwasher Donnelly?"

Oliver told them the whole story. When he had finished, co-captain Mike Graham shook his head. "It's too bad Donnelly and that Jackson kid ran away. I was planning to try out a new stranglehold today. I could've practiced on *them*!" Mike was as big and tall as Dishwasher Donnelly. In fact, his nickname was "Moose."

"We'll build Kiddo a new shed," promised Parnell. "But it'll take at least a week. Maybe more. For now, you'll have to find someplace else to keep him."

Oliver knew there was only one place he could keep Kiddo—the garage at home.

It wasn't an easy job riding home. Oliver had to steer his bike with one hand and lead Kiddo with the other. And somehow Oliver knew he wouldn't have an easy job convincing his mother to let Kiddo stay.

"I promise, Mom," Oliver pleaded. "It's just for a little while, until the football team builds a new shed. There isn't anyplace else to keep him. And it's not like he'd be staying in our house."

Oliver's mother sighed. "Okay. He can stay here. But please see that he doesn't get into my garden. And please make sure he doesn't wreck the garage."

Oliver nodded. "No problem, Mom, I'll keep him out of your way. And I'll goatproof the garage too." He let Kiddo into the garage and tied him to the workbench.

"Yap! Yap! Yap!" Pom-pom darted into the garage and snapped playfully at Kiddo's legs.

Oliver didn't want an instant replay of what had happened in the shed. He scooped up the little dog in his arms and headed for the house. "Sorry, Pom-pom, you can't play with Kiddo." Pom-pom started to whine. Oliver quickly deposited him in the kitchen. Then he went back to the garage.

Oliver moved bags, boxes, cans, and rags out of Kiddo's reach. He cleaned off the workbench. Coach Willis and Parnell were driving over later with Kiddo's snacks and water bowls and sacks of Sweet Feed.

"How about a snack?" Oliver asked. He held out a carrot. Kiddo took the carrot and munched it happily. Then he rubbed his head against Oliver's hand.

"Good boy," said Oliver, scratching the goat behind his ear. "You won't make any trouble now, will you? No more ramming into things, right?"

"*Maaaaaa*," said Kiddo, butting Oliver hard in the hip.

CHAPTER
4

Oliver braked to a full stop and jumped off his bike.

"How'd I do?" he asked Josh. "What was my time?" He had been doing practice sprints, and Josh was timing him.

Josh peered at his stopwatch. "Not too bad," he said. "You did half a mile in five minutes."

"Is that good?" asked Oliver, looking hopeful.

Josh shook his head. "You have to get it down to three minutes. C'mon, let's try it again."

It was less than a week until the bike-a-thon. Oliver wanted to get in as much practicing as he could. But he had other things to do too.

"I have to go home and feed Kiddo," he said unhappily. "And there's a math test tomorrow that I have to study for." Oliver sighed. It wasn't easy these days, fitting in chores, homework, Kiddo, and practicing.

"Oh, that test is no big deal," Josh said carelessly. Math was Josh's favorite subject. "So tomorrow," Josh continued, "we'll do some one-mile and two-mile sprints, okay?" He opened up his copy of Cycling to Win! Win! Win! "It says that 'it's a good idea to work up to the actual marathon mileage gradually. ''

Oliver nodded. "Sounds good to me," he said, hopping on his bike. He was feeling more comfortable riding it now that he knew which gears to use. But he knew he still had a lot of practicing to do before the bike-a-thon.

He and Josh were about to take off, when they suddenly heard someone screech, "Shoo! Shoo! Get out of my garbage, you . . . you . . . beast!"

Oliver covered his eyes with his hands. "Oh, no, it can't be," he groaned. "It just can't be!" He took his hand away and looked toward the house where the screeching had come from. He saw a fat woman in a bathrobe and fuzzy slippers chase a goat down her driveway.

Kiddo had done it again.

"I can't believe it!" cried Josh. "That's the third time this week Kiddo's followed us. Why did you let him out? Why didn't you tie him up?"

"I did," Oliver protested. "I've been tying him to the outside handle of the garage door so he can get some fresh air. But he's been chewing through every leash I buy." He started to pedal toward Kiddo and the woman. When he

caught up with them, he reached down and grabbed what was left of Kiddo's leash.

"Young man, is this your goat?" puffed the woman angrily. Oliver opened his mouth to reply, but the woman didn't give him a chance to say anything.

"I'll have you know I was getting ready to take a shower, when I saw this ... this ... *animal* rooting through my garbage!" Her face was purple with rage. She glared at Oliver and shook a plump finger in front of his nose. "Now, I've had just about enough of kids like you! The next time one of you juvenile delinquents pulls a prank like this, I'll call the police. Don't think I won't!"

"I'm really sorry, ma'am." Oliver used his most sincere voice. He didn't want to end up in jail with Kiddo for a cellmate. Knowing Kiddo's appetite, he'd probably eat the beds. "Please don't call the police. Honest, it won't happen again!"

"Well, see that it doesn't," snapped the woman. She turned on her heels and stomped off, muttering angrily to herself.

"Whew!" said Josh. "That was a close one!"

Oliver sighed. This was becoming a familiar scene. Yesterday Mr. Otis had yelled at him when Kiddo got into his vegetable garden. The day before, Kiddo had eaten all the tops off Mrs. Burke's morning-glories. Mrs. Burke had threatened to call Oliver's mother. And, on top of it all, Kiddo was really messing up Oliver's practice.

Josh thought so too. "I hate to say this," he said, "but at the rate we're going, we might as well forget about winning the bike-a-thon. I mean, how are we supposed to practice with that dumb goat bothering us all the time?"

"He's *not* a dumb goat," Oliver said sharply. "He just misses me, that's all."

"Okay, okay. I take it back," Josh replied. "He's not a dumb goat."

Kiddo butted into Oliver's bike, almost knocking it over.

"Well, maybe he *is* kind of stupid sometimes," Oliver admitted.

Kiddo's yellow eyes stared down at the ground. He seemed very sad.

"Oh, come on, Kiddo, I didn't mean it," Oliver said. "I guess I'm the one who's really stupid. I should know better than to leave you outside. From now on, you stay inside the garage while Josh and I practice."

"Good idea." Josh looked relieved.

"Want to come to Perkins Pet Supply with me?" Oliver asked.

"Sure," replied Josh. "What are you getting?"

"A new leash for Kiddo. What else?"

Oliver woke up the day before the race, thinking about the map of the bike-a-thon route. After breakfast he and Sam were going to ride the entire route together, with Josh as judge.

Oliver wasn't sure how fast he could ride compared to Sam. But he wanted to find out.

And this way he'd get to learn the bike-a-thon route firsthand.

It would be fun riding with Sam. But it would be practice too—practice for the big race against Rusty. Somehow he had to beat Rusty tomorrow.

Oliver glanced at the clock-radio next to his bed. Sam and Josh would be over in exactly half an hour. Oliver jumped out of bed and got dressed.

"Hey, Mom, what's for breakfast?" Oliver shouted as he bounded down the stairs. He ran into the kitchen and skidded to a stop.

His mother, wearing a huge apron, was sitting at the kitchen table. Her head was bent over several cookbooks. Pots, pans, and canisters were strewn all over the kitchen counter.

Oliver suddenly remembered that today was his mother's luncheon. Racing against Sam was definitely out—at least until the afternoon.

"Um, I'll just fix myself a bowl of cereal," he said.

Mrs. Moffitt looked up at her son. She smiled and nodded. Then she returned to her cookbooks.

Oliver sat down next to his mother and poured himself a bowl of cereal. "What kind of food are you having?" he asked curiously.

Mrs. Moffitt picked up a piece of paper and read, "Fruit salad, eggs Benedict, ham and cheese pie, corn muffins, and Aunt Joan's chocolate surprise."

Oliver raised his eyebrows. "Aunt Joan's chocolate surprise? Have I ever had that?"

His mother shook her head. "No. Your aunt

sent me the recipe yesterday. It's really just a chocolate meringue pie."

"It sounds terrific!" Oliver said. "But what's the surprise part?"

Mrs. Moffitt rolled her eyes. "Getting it to come out right!" she said. "Meringue pies can be a little tricky."

"Don't worry, Mom," Oliver said. "It'll be perfect!"

"Thanks." His mother smiled. She stood up. "Well, I'd better get started. Are you ready to be my assistant chef and party-giver?"

"Sure." Oliver nodded. "But first I'd better feed Kiddo." He ran out the kitchen door. Just as he was opening the garage door, Josh and Sam rode up the driveway.

"I have some bad news for you guys," Oliver said. He told them about his mother's luncheon and how he had to help out. "But I can race this afternoon," he finished. "Can you both come back after lunch?"

Sam shook her head. "I'm going downtown with my mother." She made a face. "I have to buy a dress for my piano recital." Sam hated to wear dresses.

"I'll be back," Josh promised. "We can do some last-minute sprints."

Around the corner came a familiar, unwelcome sight—Rusty on his bicycle.

"Uh-oh, here comes trouble," Sam said. "I wonder how many mean pills he took today."

"Hi there, fellow sports fans," Rusty said, grinning. He hopped off his bike.

"What do you want, Rusty?" Oliver snapped. "Why don't you leave us alone?"

Rusty raised his eyebrows. "Don't get mad, pal. I just came over to wish you luck tomorrow." His grin widened.

"Yeah?" Oliver gave him a hard look. Whenever Rusty acted like a nice guy, it was time to really watch out.

"Yeah!" Rusty gave a loud hoot of laughter. "I mean, you're gonna need all the luck you can get! Ha! Ha! Ha! Ha!" He slapped his leg and laughed even louder.

Oliver rolled his eyes. It was just like Rusty to wish a person good luck and really not mean it at all.

Rusty stopped laughing and peered into the garage. "Hey, there's my pal the goat!" he exclaimed. He walked into the garage. "How're you doing, goat?"

"You leave him alone!" Oliver shouted, hurrying into the garage. Josh and Sam followed him.

Rusty ignored Oliver. He started to tug on Kiddo's leash, then jumped as Kiddo butted at him. Oliver could see that the goat really hated Rusty.

"If you don't get out of here *now*, I'll . . ." Oliver started. Then he stopped. He wasn't sure what he was going to do. He just knew he was getting madder by the minute.

"You'll what?" sneered Rusty. "Go get your mommy?"

That was the last straw. Oliver had really had

enough of Rusty. He clenched his fists and shouted, "I'll race you!"

"Huh?" Rusty turned to Oliver. "Race *me*?"

Oliver nodded. "That's right. Here and now. Just the two of us." He glared at Rusty. *"Well?"*

Rusty glared back at him. "Okay, Moffitt, you're *on!*"

"Oh, no," Josh groaned. "Oliver, don't do it! You're not ready for Rusty!"

But it was too late to back out now.

Oliver and Rusty agreed to race from the stop sign at the corner of Oliver's street to the gas station, about a mile down the road. Both Josh and Sam were judges. Rusty had insisted on having two judges.

At the starting signal, the boys took off, each pumping as hard as he could.

Josh and Sam rode alongside them. "Come on, Oliver!" shouted Josh.

"Look out!" screeched Sam. "Pothole ahead!"

Oliver and Rusty neatly swerved around the hole, Oliver to the right of it, Rusty to the left. Oliver grinned as he thought of the last time he'd met up with that pothole.

They were neck-and-neck when Oliver saw the gas station looming ahead. He changed gears, lifted himself off the seat of his bike, and bore down on the pedals, giving himself an extra spurt of speed. Oliver glided past Rusty into the station, bumping over the rubber hose on the ground. *Ding, ding.* The race was over. Oliver braked to a stop.

"I can't believe it!" cried Josh, slapping him on the back. "You won! You beat Rusty!"

"Congratulations, Oliver," Sam added. She turned to Rusty. "Well, how does it feel to be a loser—*pal*?" she asked him, grinning broadly.

Rusty glared at her. Then he glared at Oliver. His face was dark with anger. "I'll get you for this, Moffitt," he said softly. "You'll be sorry you ever raced against me."

"What are you going to do, tell your mommy?" Oliver asked. He was too excited to be cautious with Rusty.

Rusty smiled slowly. It wasn't a nice smile. "You'll see," he said menacingly. "You'll see." He hopped back onto his bike and rode off.

Sam watched him go, her hands on her hips. "What a sore loser," she said, shaking her head.

"He'll be even sorer tomorrow," joked Josh. They all laughed.

"Oh, no!" Oliver exclaimed suddenly. "Mom's lunch!" He'd just remembered that he was supposed to be at home helping his mother with her luncheon. And he'd forgotten to feed Kiddo! He jumped on his bike.

"See you guys later," he called.

"Way to go, champ!" Josh yelled after him. "Tomorrow's a piece of cake!"

Two unfamiliar cars were parked in the driveway when Oliver got home. Mrs. Moffitt's guests had arrived!

Oliver saw that the garage door was still open.

But there was no goat tied to the workbench. Kiddo was gone!

And this time Kiddo hadn't chewed through his leash. The leash was gone too. Kiddo must still be wearing it.

"Dishwasher Donnelly!" Oliver groaned. "I've been working so hard, I forgot all about him!"

Oliver rushed wildly out of the garage. He checked the front yard. Then he looked in the Lawrences' front yard, next door. There was no sign of Kiddo.

Which way could a goat-napper go? Oliver looked up and down the street. Should he call the police? What if the Dishwasher got Kiddo in trouble? Or even worse, hurt him?

All of a sudden he heard a piercing scream. It came from the Moffitts' back yard.

"I'm coming!" Oliver yelled as he charged into the back yard. Then he froze. Mrs. Kirkby was lying in the middle of Mrs. Moffitt's autumn garden. And right beside her was Kiddo, nibbling at a chrysanthemum.

"Hello, Oliver!" Mrs. Kirkby got up on her knees and waved.

Mrs. Moffitt came running out of the back door. She was holding a coffeepot.

"What on earth . . . ?" she said, staring at the scene in the garden. She set the coffeepot down on a lawn chair and rushed over to Mrs. Kirkby. Meanwhile, Oliver tried to pull Kiddo out of the garden.

Mr. Kirkby and Mr. and Mrs. Caplan also came out of the house. Mr. Kirkby had a dish in

his hands—the eggs Benedict Mrs. Moffitt had been working on. "Florence!" he called. "What are you doing?"

At that moment Pom-pom dashed out the door, barking loudly. He brushed against the chair, knocking over the coffeepot. Then he ran between Mr. Kirkby's legs and headed toward Kiddo. Mr. Kirkby lost his balance, and his plate went flying, dropping eggs and sauce all over his wife's blouse.

Oliver covered his eyes with his hands and shook his head. "Disaster," he murmured. "Total disaster."

Mrs. Moffitt quickly scooped up the frisking dog and held him tightly. "Mrs. Kirkby, I'm so sorry about this." She could hardly be heard over Pom-pom's squeals.

"Oh, it's nothing." Mrs. Kirkby laughed as she struggled to get up, helped by her husband and Mr. Caplan. "I just bent down to get a closer look at your lovely chrysanthemums, Ellen. I guess my backside was too tempting a target for our friend here." She pointed to Kiddo.

"Oliver," said Mrs. Moffitt grimly. "I think we'd better have a little talk."

Oliver had just managed to pull Kiddo out of the garden. It hadn't been easy. The goat had discovered the fabric flower on the tip of Mrs. Kirkby's shoe. He kept leaning over to eat it.

"Now, now, Ellen, I'm perfectly all right." Mrs. Kirkby had gotten to her feet and was brushing bits of dirt and leaves off her dark blue skirt.

Mrs. Caplan kindly took Pom-pom inside.

Mrs. Moffitt cleared her throat. "Why don't you *all* go back into the living room and have some coff—" she saw the overturned coffeepot— "—and I'll join you in just a minute," she said, smiling brightly. The four guests headed for the house.

Mrs. Moffitt stopped smiling. She turned to Oliver and said in a stern voice, "Young man, I want to talk to you in the garage. Right now!"

Oliver tried to explain what had happened. "Don't you see, Mom?" he pleaded. "I had to race Rusty. I just *had* to. Don't you understand?"

"What I understand," said his mother, "is that when I needed help, you were nowhere to be found! Rather than helping, you created problems. You *knew* how unpredictable Kiddo could be. And, worst of all, you broke a promise. You said you'd stay home and help me out. I'm very disappointed in you."

Oliver looked down at the floor. He hated it when his mother was disappointed in him. All the happiness he had felt after beating Rusty was gone.

"I'm sorry, Mom," he said. "I guess I just got carried away with the bike-a-thon and Rusty and everything." He looked at his mother. "I'll go and apologize to Mrs. Kirkby too."

Mrs. Moffitt nodded. "I'm glad to hear it," she told him. "And after you do that, I would like you to spend the afternoon in your room."

"But, Mom!" protested Oliver. "What about the bike-a-thon? I have to practice this afternoon!"

"I'm sorry, Oliver, but that's my final word on the subject," his mother said firmly. "And now I have to get back to my guests." She turned away from him and marched out of the garage.

Oliver slowly tied Kiddo to the workbench. Then he gave the goat some Sweet Feed. He had stepped out of the garage and was closing the door, when a horrible thought suddenly struck him.

What if his mother were angry enough to ground him for the rest of the weekend?

What if she decided to punish him by making him drop out of the bike-a-thon? Then Oliver would lose by default. And Rusty would probably win.

"Mom wouldn't do that to me," Oliver said to himself. "She *couldn't* do that to me. Could she?"

Oliver lay in bed that night. He couldn't get to sleep. He kept thinking about how horrible it would be if he couldn't ride in the bike-a-thon.

His mother was angry, Oliver could tell. She had brought up a lunch tray, put it on his desk, and left the room without saying a word. During dinner she had been very quiet. And she had just said "Good night" when Oliver told her that he was going upstairs to work on his book report.

"I really messed up this time," Oliver sighed. He turned over onto his stomach and tried to go to sleep.

Suddenly Oliver heard a strange sound. He sat up in bed. It was coming from the back yard. Something was moving out there.

Staring into the darkness, Oliver had a terrible thought. What if Kiddo had gotten loose again? But he couldn't. Oliver had locked the garage door.

The faint noise came again. Oliver went to the bedroom window. He strained his eyes. There, down by the back-yard fence, a shadow was moving.

A shadow on two legs.

Oliver froze. A burglar?

The shadow moved up to the house, peering into the kitchen windows. Then it headed over to the garage.

Oliver knew he should be yelling for help. He opened his mouth, but no sound came out. He tried to run, but his feet were stuck to the floor.

The burglar must have been good with locks. Oliver soon heard the sound of the garage door being opened.

Then he heard a sound that was very familiar. *"Ah-choo!"*

Oliver knew that sneeze anywhere. "Oh, no! Not again!" he thought.

"C'mon, you dumb goat. Let me—*ah-choo!* —get this knot . . . *yow!*"

The night air erupted in a series of loud

sneezes, followed by cries like "Ow!" "Yipe!" and "Yow!"

Oliver ran to his closet and quickly struggled into some clothes. Then the leaves on the tree by his window began to shake. Someone was climbing up!

Oliver peered out the window. Down in the back yard, Kiddo alertly paced around the tree, looking up.

The leaf-swishing on the tree got louder. Then a face appeared on the other side of the window.

Of course, it was Dishwasher Donnelly.

Oliver breathed a sigh of relief. Well, he was right. It wasn't a burglar. Well, not a *real* burglar anyway. Just a goat-napper who was allergic to goats.

The Dishwasher clung to his tree branch, staring at Oliver with his mouth open.

"Um, uh, nice tree ya got here, kid," the Dishwasher finally said.

Oliver slammed his window shut. Dishwasher Donnelly jumped back.

Crack! went the branch he was perched on.

"AAAAAaaaaaaaah!" went Dishwasher Donnelly as he fell.

Thump! went the Dishwasher as he hit the ground.

"Oliver!" shouted Mrs. Moffitt. "What's going on? Are you all right?"

"Uh, I'm okay, Mom," Oliver called out. "That was just Doctor Destructo on the radio. He was giving one of his famous bloodcurdling midnight yells."

"Well, turn that radio off and go to bed! It's late!"

Oliver looked out the window to see the Dishwasher get up from the ground—just in time to be butted by Kiddo.

He sneaked downstairs, ran outside, and got the goat's leash just as Dishwasher Donnelly limped away. Kiddo wanted to chase the Dishwasher, but Oliver finally managed to get him into the garage again. He gave the goat an extra snack of Sweet Feed.

As Oliver went back to bed, he couldn't help grinning. At least there was one person who'd had a worse day than he had.

CHAPTER
5

It was early Sunday morning, the day of the bike-a-thon.

Oliver was still asleep. He was having a nightmare. In it, Mrs. Kirkby was wearing a three-piece dark blue suit and a hat made out of chrysanthemums. She was holding a microphone.

"Aaand, coming into the final stretch, it's Rusty in the lead," she announced. "No, wait a minute, folks, it's Oliver in the lead! No, it's Rusty . . . no, it's Sam . . . no, it's Oliver . . . yes, it's . . ." Suddenly Oliver's mother stepped into the dream. "Young man," she said, "you're grounded! Go to your room!"

Oliver woke up with a start. "Wow!" he said into the pillow. "That was the worst dream I ever had!"

He sat up and looked around his room to

make sure he wasn't still dreaming. He breathed a sigh of relief. Everything looked normal. A little messy, but normal.

But Oliver was worried. What if part of his dream came true? The part about being grounded?

Oliver got dressed and went downstairs. His mother was sitting at the kitchen table. She was drinking a glass of orange juice and reading the paper. She didn't look up.

"Um, morning, Mom," Oliver said, sitting down next to her. She didn't say anything. "You're not still mad at me, are you?" he asked in a small voice.

Mrs. Moffitt looked at him and sighed. "No, I'm not still mad at you."

"Whew!" breathed Oliver. "That's a relief! I was afraid you were going to ground me!" He slumped back in his chair. "I even had a bad dream about it!"

"Well, to tell you the truth, I had thought of grounding you today," admitted his mother.

Oliver's face fell. "I knew it."

"But I decided that it really wouldn't be fair, and that sending you to your room was punishment enough," Mrs. Moffitt said.

"Oh, it was, it was," Oliver said solemnly.

"But I hope you realize now what it means to be a responsible person," his mother added sternly. "And that you can't let people down when they're relying on you. And that goes for animals too!"

Oliver nodded emphatically. "I understand,

Mom, I really do. And I'm sorry again for what happened. I shouldn't have let Rusty Jackson get my goat." He groaned at the bad joke. "Actually I should have let my goat get Rusty Jackson. Kiddo really hates him."

Mrs. Moffitt laughed. "Well, it's nice to know you two have something in common." She stood up. "I accept your apology. Now, what would you like for breakfast? You've got a busy day ahead of you!"

"Just toast and cereal," insisted Oliver. "Josh says it's not a good idea to eat too much before a big race." He thought for a minute. He was pretty hungry. "But I guess it wouldn't hurt to have a scrambled egg and sausage too," he added quickly.

After breakfast Oliver ran outside to make sure that his bike was in perfect working order. He checked the gears, pedals, tires, and seat. He even tested the lights, though he knew he wouldn't need them.

Oliver looked at his watch. Josh and Sam would be arriving at any minute. They were going to ride over to the starting point together. Oliver figured he'd better give Kiddo his breakfast before they showed up.

Mrs. Moffitt came outside. She put an arm around Oliver's shoulder and gave him a quick hug.

"Good luck," she said. "I'll be there rooting for you. But if you don't see me right away when you get there, don't panic. I've got some work to finish up first."

"Okay, Mom." Oliver nodded. Then a thought struck him. "Hey, Mom, is it okay if I leave the garage door open just a crack? So Kiddo can have some fresh air?"

"That's fine with me," his mother agreed. "I'll close the door and lock it before I leave."

Just then Sam and Josh pulled into the driveway. Both of them were wearing white sweat shirts that had BIKE-A-THON printed on them in big red letters.

"Hey, where'd you get those neat sweat shirts?" Oliver asked.

Josh grinned. "My mother had them made for everyone in our class." Mrs. Burns was their class mother this term. "Here's yours, Oliver. I hope it fits."

Oliver took off his lightweight nylon jacket and put on the the sweat shirt. It fit perfectly.

"Now you really look like you're part of a racing team," said Mrs. Moffitt. She turned to go back into the house.

"Good luck, everybody," she said with a smile. "Ride like the wind!"

"That reminds me," said Josh. He licked his finger and held it up. "No wind velocity today."

"So what?" asked Sam.

"Is that good or bad?" Oliver asked anxiously. The whole time they were training together, Josh had never said anything about wind velocity. Oliver didn't even know what wind velocity was!

Josh shrugged. "It depends. Sometimes it's good if there's a fast tail wind behind you to give you that little extra push while you're riding."

"Oh," said Oliver glumly.

"On the other hand," Josh continued, "if you have to ride *into* the wind, it can slow you down."

"Oh!" Oliver said brightly. He felt much better. He didn't want anything to slow him down today.

"Well, since there isn't any wind at all, why worry about it?" Sam said impatiently. She glanced at her watch.

"Good point." Josh nodded. "Forget I even brought it up."

"Come on, you guys," Oliver said. "Help me feed Kiddo. Then we'd better get going, or else wind or no wind, they'll disqualify us!"

When Oliver, Sam, and Josh arrived at the starting line, Coach Josh whispered some last-minute racing tips to Oliver. Then he slapped Oliver on the back and made the thumbs-up sign. "Good luck!" he cried as he ran to take his place on the sidelines.

Sam surveyed the scene. Then she gave Oliver a nudge. "Look," she said, pointing. "There's Rusty. But I don't see Jay anywhere. Do you think he dropped out?"

"Who knows," Oliver replied with a shrug. He didn't care about Jay. The person he had to beat was Rusty.

Sam turned to Jennifer, who was waiting next to them. "Hey, Jennifer," she said suddenly. "How come you're not wearing a bike-a-thon sweat shirt like the rest of us?" Jennifer was wearing her favorite Purple Worms sweat shirt over a pair of purple velour sweat pants. A purple headband and pink sneakers completed her outfit.

Jennifer tossed her head. "It was the wrong color," she said. "Besides, this is my lucky shirt!"

"You look like a grape," Matthew commented. "A huge grape."

Jennifer gave him a dirty look.

"Psst," hissed Kim. "Here comes Mr. Thompson."

Mr. Thompson, the principal of Bartlett Woods Elementary School, was walking up the steps of the judges' stand. He adjusted the microphone, cleared his throat, and started to speak.

"Ladies and gentlemen, boys and girls, parents, teachers, and friends," he announced. "I want to welcome you all to the first Bartlett Woods Elementary School Bike-a-thon for charity. As you know, our fair city has always . . ."

Oliver wished Mr. Thompson would hurry up and finish his speech so they could get on with the race. He was starting to feel nervous. Something was doing somersaults inside his stomach.

"Just a few butterflies," he reassured himself. "Nothing to worry about."

Finally Mr. Thompson came to the end of his speech. ". . . And now, racers, my assistant principal, Ms. Simpson, will be attaching numbers to your bikes. The numbers are adhesive, so they can't fall off. Good luck, one and all!"

"Thirteen!" exclaimed Oliver when it was his turn to receive a number. "Please, may I have another number," he begged Ms. Simpson. "Any number but thirteen!"

Ms. Simpson shook her head. "Sorry, Oliver, this is the only number I have left." She slapped the piece of paper onto his back and scurried away.

Oliver looked over at Rusty. On his back was the number one.

"Oh, great," Oliver said.

"Some people think thirteen is a lucky number," Sam told him.

"Yeah. I'll bet," Oliver replied glumly.

"All right, racers, take your places!" Mr. Thompson announced.

Oliver put one foot on the pedal of his bike, adjusted the gears, and leaned over. Suddenly he heard someone yelling his name. He looked over at the sidelines. His mother was standing there, shouting "Oliver!" and waving her arms frantically. She was also shouting something that sounded like "Go! Go!" but the crowd was so noisy, Oliver couldn't be sure.

Oliver grinned and waved at his mother. Then he leaned over the handlebars again.

Bang! The starting gun went off.

Oliver pedaled steadily. He kept his eyes on the road, but he also glanced at his fellow racers out of the corner of his eye from time to time. He wanted to know where they were so he wouldn't bump into them.

"It's a good thing I studied that map so carefully," he thought as he rounded a corner. He knew there was going to be a steep hill ahead.

He shifted gears, pumped up the hill easily, and glided swiftly down the other side.

After a few miles he checked his speedometer. That was one of the nicest features of his new bike.

"Only four miles to go!" Oliver said to himself. He started to pedal a little harder.

By the fifth mile Oliver had passed all of his classmates except Sam. Then he passed most of the sixth-graders.

By the sixth mile he had passed Greg Potter, a sixth-grader, and Rusty.

He was way ahead of Rusty when he caught up to Sam. She glanced at him quickly and grinned.

Oliver grinned back. But his smile froze as he suddenly spotted two familiar shapes ahead. One was Jay Goodman, giving the thumbs-up sign and grinning from ear to ear.

The other shape was—Kiddo!

Oliver quickly realized what his mother had been shouting. "The goat's gone! The goat's gone! The goat's gone!" He also figured that Jay must have sneaked into the garage, stolen Kiddo, and brought him to the race. It was all part of Rusty's revenge plan. If Oliver dropped out, Rusty would have to win!

Oliver pulled up alongside Jay and Kiddo. "You creep!" he yelled. "You goat-napping creep!" He grabbed at Kiddo's leash. "Let him go!"

Jay jerked the leash away from Oliver. "Not until the race is over," he sneered. "You can have Kiddo back when everyone's crossed the finish line except *you*!"

Oliver lurched forward. This time he managed to get his hand on the leash. He pulled at it. Jay pulled too.

"Forget it, Moffitt!" Jay shouted. "I'm not letting go of this leash!"

"Having a little trouble, pal?" a voice called out.

Oliver whirled around and saw Rusty riding toward them. "Now who's got the goat, Moffitt?" he shouted gleefully. Then he started to sing "Old MacDonald Had a Farm" in a mocking voice, laughing as he sang.

Kiddo lifted up his head sharply. When he heard the song and saw who was singing it, he charged. The leash flew out of Oliver's hand. Jay fell on his face.

"*Maaa!*" bawled Kiddo. He lowered his head into butting position and took off at top speed after his old enemy, Rusty Jackson.

Oliver clapped his hand to his forehead. "Oh, no, what do I do *now*?"

Then he shook his head. "No problem. There's just one thing to do." Oliver hopped on his bike and pedaled as fast as he could after Rusty and Kiddo.

When he caught up to them, he saw Kiddo butt at the wheel of Rusty's bike. "Hey!" Rusty cried. "Cut that out!" But Kiddo kept right on butting. Finally Rusty lost his balance. He and his bike spilled over onto the grass. Rusty untangled himself from the bike and crawled to his knees. He looked totally dazed.

Meanwhile Oliver had thought of the only possible way he could stay in the race. He leaned over and grabbed Kiddo's leash.

"Okay, Kiddo," he said. "Listen to this!" He started to sing "Old MacDonald" as fast and as loudly as he could.

It worked! Kiddo ran alongside Oliver as Oliver puffed out the song.

> Old MacDonald had a farm,
> Keep go-i-i-ing!
> And on that farm, he had a goat,
> Don't let me down now, Kid-do!

Kiddo didn't seem to mind the fact that Oliver had changed the words of the song slightly. He kept running as Oliver sang.

Soon Oliver had caught up to the sixth-graders again. They jerked up their heads and stared at him as he belted out his version of the song.

Still singing, Oliver managed to pass Greg Potter. He could see Sam up ahead. She was almost at the finish line!

Oliver pumped harder and sang louder. Perspiration was pouring down his forehead. He was exhausted from singing, pedaling, steering his bike with one hand, and holding Kiddo's leash with the other.

But he couldn't give up now! They were almost there! He gritted his teeth and bore down on the pedals with all his might.

Then, before he knew it, he was alongside Sam.

The three of them—Sam, Oliver, and Kiddo—streaked across the finish line together! It was a tie!

Oliver braked to a stop, puffing and gasping. He couldn't believe it! He'd won the bike-a-thon!

The crowd surged forward, Josh and Mrs. Moffitt in the lead. Oliver's mother gave him a big hug. Then she hugged Sam too. The Lawrences ran up to congratulate their daughter. "We won! We won!" shouted Josh. He slapped Oliver on the back. "I knew we could do it!"

A few minutes later Sam and Oliver were led up to the judges' platform to receive their trophies. Oliver brought Kiddo onto the platform too. After Mr. Thompson said a few words of congratulations, he gave Sam her trophy. Then he turned to Oliver and smiled.

"On behalf of the Bartlett Woods Elementary School Bike-a-thon," he said, handing Oliver his trophy, "I want to thank you, Oliver, for making this a very exciting race."

The crowd applauded loudly.

Oliver took the trophy. Then he leaned over and gave Kiddo a pat on the back.

"Don't thank me." He grinned at Mr. Thompson. "Thank Kiddo!"

CHAPTER
6

The next morning before school Oliver sat at the kitchen table and gazed at the trophy in front of him. The sunlight glinted on the little silver bicycle. Oliver sighed contentedly.

"Can you take your eyes off that trophy long enough to have some breakfast?" teased his mother. She set down a plate of French toast swimming in syrup.

"French toast!" exclaimed Oliver. "My favorite!" He took a bite. It tasted delicious.

"Don't forget about sharing your trophy with Josh," reminded Mrs. Moffitt. "After all, he was your coach."

Oliver nodded. "Don't worry, Mom," he said. "We figured it all out. I'm keeping it for a month. Then Josh gets to keep it for a month. Then I get to keep it for a month, and then he—"

"I get the idea," his mother interrupted, her eyes twinkling.

Oliver had finished his plate of French toast and was about to ask for seconds, when there was a knock at the kitchen door.

Oliver looked up and saw Parnell standing outside. With him was a tall man whom Oliver had never seen before.

When Oliver opened the door, Parnell greeted Mrs. Moffitt. Then he said, "Oliver, Mrs. Moffitt, this is Seth MacDonald. He's the owner of Mac-Donald's Petting Farm. Kiddo belongs to him."

"Won't you both come in?" asked Mrs. Moffitt. Parnell and Mr. MacDonald stepped inside the kitchen.

"Nice to meet you, Oliver, Mrs. Moffitt." Mr. MacDonald smiled as he shook both their hands.

"Mr. MacDonald's farm is moving to another state," Parnell said.

"That's right," Mr. MacDonald said, nodding. "So I'm here to take Kiddo off your hands."

"Oh!" said Oliver. "Well, I'll miss him. He and I have been through a lot together." Oliver felt sad at the thought of saying good-bye to Kiddo. But Kiddo *had* been kind of a handful to take care of. So he was a little relieved too.

"Yes, Parnell told me all about your adventures with Kiddo." Mr. MacDonald smiled. "Including the bike-a-thon and 'Old MacDonald Had a Farm.' By the way, I was the one who trained him to run whenever he hears that song."

"He sure knows how to run, all right," exclaimed Oliver. "He's got to be the fastest goat around!"

"You may be right," Mr. MacDonald agreed with a smile.

"Mr. Thompson, the principal of my school, said he was sorry that Kiddo couldn't have a trophy too," Oliver explained. "But it wouldn't have been fair because he wasn't riding a bike."

"I don't think I could train Kiddo to do *that!*" Mr. MacDonald chuckled.

Oliver took Mr. MacDonald and Parnell out to the garage. Mr. MacDonald greeted Kiddo affectionately. The goat seemed happy to see him.

"Kiddo looks healthy and contented," Mr. MacDonald said, turning to Oliver. "You did a fine job taking care of him."

Oliver felt his face grow warm with pleasure. "Oh, it's all in a day's work," he said modestly.

He knelt down and gave Kiddo a hug around the neck. "So long, Kiddo," he whispered. The goat turned his head slightly and gave Oliver's shoulder a gentle bump.

"I'll miss you too, pal," Oliver said sadly. He got up, untied Kiddo's leash, and silently handed it to Mr. MacDonald. The man gave him a sympathetic look. He seemed to understand how Oliver was feeling.

"Don't worry," he said. "We love all our animals at MacDonald's. And Kiddo's one of my all-time favorites. He'll be well looked after."

"I know." Oliver nodded.

The three of them loaded the sacks of Sweet Feed into the back of Mr. MacDonald's van.

After Mr. MacDonald led Kiddo into the back of the van, he hopped into the front seat.

"Thanks again!" he called out to Oliver. "And if you ever want a summer job at MacDonald's Petting Farm, drop me a line. Parnell knows our new address!"

"I'll keep that in mind!" Oliver replied as Mr. MacDonald drove away.

"Oh, wow, I almost forgot," Parnell said, digging into the pocket of his jeans. He pulled out a folded-up paper. "Here's your check for taking care of Kiddo."

Oliver took the check and read the amount. It wasn't as much as he would have earned taking care of Kiddo for the whole football season. But it was just enough to pay his mother back for his new bike.

"Thanks." Oliver smiled. Then he suddenly thought of something. "Hey, Parnell," he said, "the Tigers don't have a mascot anymore!"

"Oh, yes, we do," said Parnell. "We've got a terrific mascot." He smiled mysteriously.

"What kind of animal is it?" Oliver asked curiously.

"You'll see him on Saturday," answered Parnell. "You're coming to the game, aren't you?"

"You bet!" Oliver said. "I want to see you guys crush the Raiders and win the county championship."

"Meet me at the shed before the pep rally," Parnell told him. "We just finished rebuilding it. Our new mascot really likes it!"

"I'll be there!" Oliver promised. He said a

quick good-bye to Parnell and hurried off to school.

The first person Oliver saw when he stepped inside the school was Rusty Jackson. He was by himself. Jay was nowhere in sight.

"Well, if it isn't the bike-a-thon champ," Rusty said, sneering.

Oliver ignored him. He marched past Rusty down the hall. Rusty followed him.

"How does it feel to be a cheater?" he said.

Oliver stopped short. He turned around and stared at Rusty. "What are you talking about?" he demanded. "Why am I a cheater?"

"Oh, come off it, Moffitt," Rusty said impatiently. "You could never have beaten me if that stupid goat hadn't hit my bike. Face it, pal, you won that race unfairly."

"Look who's talking about cheating and fairness!" Oliver said angrily. "The goat wouldn't have been there if you hadn't told Jay to steal Kiddo. You were trying to get me to drop out. That was a really creepy thing to do!"

"Yeah, well, you're not going to tell anyone about that, are you?" Rusty mumbled.

Oliver laughed. "Everybody saw Jay with Kiddo!" He shook his head. "But I think your stealing Kiddo cancels out Kiddo butting you. Face it, Rusty. We're even—and I beat you, fair and square!"

They had gotten to the door of Oliver's classroom.

"Okay, okay, maybe you did," Rusty admitted grudgingly. Then a gleam came into his eye. "But maybe the next time you won't be so lucky. You can't beat me all the time, Moffitt. Remember that." He sauntered away, smiling to himself.

Oliver shook his head slowly. Rusty would never change. Oliver opened the door, stepped inside the noisy classroom, and hurried to his seat just as the bell rang.

"Class, class, settle down," said Ms. Callahan. "Now that we're all here"—she looked at Oliver, who sank down in his seat—"I'd like to thank you all for participating in the bike-a-thon. It was a big success. We raised a great deal of money for charity."

Oliver and his classmates gave a loud cheer.

Ms. Callahan smiled. "I also think our two winners deserve some appreciation, don't you? Let's have a big cheer for Oliver Moffitt and Samantha Lawrence! Stand up, you two!"

Oliver and Sam stood up, grinning from ear to ear as the class cheered and clapped.

When the cheering had died down, Oliver said loyally, "And Josh rates a cheer too! He was my coach. I couldn't have won the race without him!"

Everybody cheered Josh, who looked embarrassed but pleased.

The first class of the morning was music. "You all seem pretty wide awake to me," Ms. Callahan teased. "But let's sing the eye-opener I had in mind anyway. Please turn to page twenty-three of your songbooks."

"*That* baby song?" said Matthew, who had found the page first.

Oliver turned to page twenty-three. He looked at the song title and swallowed hard. Then he raised his hand.

"Yes, Oliver?" said Ms. Callahan. "Is this song too babyish for you too?"

"It's not that, exactly," Oliver gulped. "It's just that . . . what I mean is . . . do you think we could sing something else? *Anything* except 'Old MacDonald Had a Farm'!"

Everyone laughed. Then Ms. Callahan said, "Instead of a song, let's have one last cheer. For Kiddo!"

The class cheered, Oliver the loudest of all.

Saturday was the county championship game. Oliver and Sam headed across the junior high football field toward the shed. On the way they passed Kim, Jennifer, and a bunch of cheerleaders practicing.

> Smash 'em, bash 'em, squash 'em hard!
> Squeeze 'em up, beat 'em down,
> Win that yard!

Oliver shook his head. "That's some cheer."

"I can't wait to see the Tigers' new mascot," Sam said excitedly. "What do you think it is? A Great Dane? Another goat? It couldn't be a *real* tiger, could it?"

"We'll find out soon enough," Oliver replied. "Here comes Parnell."

Parnell ran up beside them. "Are you guys ready to see the greatest mascot *ever*?" he asked.

Oliver and Sam nodded impatiently. "Follow me," said Parnell.

Suddenly they heard a loud bellowing noise coming from inside the shed.

"Your new mascot is an *elephant*?" asked Sam, wrinkling her forehead.

The door of the shed burst open and Dishwasher Donnelly rushed out, screaming, *"Yaaaaaah!* A snake! There's a snake in there!" He jumped over the fence and ran down the road, still screaming.

Oliver grinned at Parnell. "It's Squeeze Me!" he cried.

"Right!" Parnell smiled. "We decided that my boa constrictor would make the perfect mascot."

"He *is* the perfect mascot," chuckled Oliver. "Especially for a snake in the grass like Dishwasher Donnelly!"